Rainy Day Play Book

By Susan Young
with Marion Conger & Natalie Young

Illustrated by Ib Ohlsson

Golden Press · New York
Western Publishing Company, Inc.   Racine, Wisconsin

D1093630

"It's raining," said Peter as he looked out the window. "We'll have to stay inside."

"What will we do all day?" asked Abby.

"There are lots of things you can do on a rainy day," Mother said.

"But we're tired of playing with all our old toys," Peter complained.

"Why not exchange toys?" asked Mother.

"That's a great idea!" exclaimed Abby. "Let's have a toy-trading store."

Peter and Abby each got a few toys and put them on the playroom table. Abby exchanged her magic ring for Peter's pen that could write in four different colors. Peter exchanged his xylophone for Abby's clown puppet.

"This is almost as much fun as getting new toys!" said Peter.

They played with their new toys for a while. Then Abby told Peter, "I'm going to write you a message with my new pen. I know a special way to send it, too. Come on, I'll show you."

Abby tied a string to the leg of Peter's bed.
It stretched out to the hall. She wrote a message and folded it very small. Then she at-
tached a paper clip to it, and slipped it onto
the string. Holding the string, Abby raised her
arm. The message slid down to Peter.

Peter wrote Abby a message. He untied his
end of the string and held it up in the air.
"Hold your end of the string all the way down
on the floor," he called to Abby. He slid the
message down the string to Abby.

Peter's message said, "Let's pretend we're at the library."

He and Abby chose their favorite books and put them on the table.

"I'll be librarian," Peter said. He got an envelope and some small white cards. He wrote the name of a book on each card and put the cards

in the books. "The library is open," he said.

"Do you have any stories about animals?"
Abby asked.

"Here's a book about the zoo," said Peter. He
took the card out of the book, wrote Abby's
name on it, and put it in the envelope.

Then it was Abby's turn to be librarian. Peter came to the library dressed as a daddy. Abby helped him find a book of bedtime stories.

Abby and Peter were reading their books when the doorbell rang.

Mark and Betty had come to visit.

Betty had brought some paper. "Let's make snowflake cutouts," she said.

Each child folded a sheet of paper in half, in half again, and in half once more. Then Betty showed them how to cut out squares, diamonds, and triangles. When they unfolded the papers, each had a lovely snowflake design.

Mark and Abby taped their snowflakes to the window. Betty and Peter put theirs on top of a sheet of plain paper and used crayons to color the cut-out places. "The designs are so pretty!" Abby said.

"I know how to make pretty designs with paint," said Mark. He folded a sheet of paper in half, then opened it up. He dripped blobs of paint onto one half of the paper. Then he folded the other half over and pressed down

hard with his hand. When he unfolded the
paper, there was a beautiful design on it.

"The design on one half looks like the one
on the other half, only backwards!" said Peter.

"It's called a mirror print," Mark said.

"Let's have a car show," said Abby when they
had all finished making their mirror prints.

"Where will we get the cars?" asked Betty.

"We can cut pictures of them out of maga-
zines," Abby replied. "Mother saves old ones
for Peter and me."

Abby and Peter cut out pictures of cars and
put them all around the room. Meanwhile,
Betty and Mark cut out pictures of people.

They had a whole family: mother, father, two grandmas and grandpas, a big sister, and a baby brother.

"The car show has begun," Peter and Abby announced.

The paper family came to the show and admired all the cars.

After the car show was over, Abby and Peter cut out more pictures of people while Mark and Betty cut out pictures of animals, furniture, houses, and food. They got some paper, pasted a few pictures on each sheet, and wrote a little story on each page. Then they put the pages together and made four little storybooks.

"Who would like to help me bake some cookies?" Mother called from the kitchen.

"I would!" cried all four children at once.

Mark and Abby measured the flour and sugar, Betty put in the raisins, and Peter put the dough on the cookie sheet.

While the cookies were in the oven, Mother showed the children how to make dough faces.

She helped them mix two cups of flour, a half cup of salt, and three-quarters of a cup of water in a big bowl until they had a ball of smooth dough.

The children rolled pieces of dough into little balls, then flattened them into circles. They rolled strands of dough to make hair, and

shaped dough bits to make eyes, noses, and mouths. They made freckles by pressing pencil points into the dough. Finally, they made a hole at the top of each face.

"In a few days they will be completely dry," said Mother. "Then we can put string through the holes and hang them up."

"We made so many nice things today," Abby
said. "Let's have a fair."

The others thought it was a wonderful idea.
They tidied up the playroom. Then they set out
the mirror prints, snowflake cutouts, little storybooks, paper cars, and paper family. Abby and
Peter reopened the toy exchange and the library.

When the fair was ready, they invited Mother in. She read the storybooks and chose a snowflake cutout for the kitchen window.

"How beautiful everything is!" she said. "You have all been so busy today that you must be very hungry. Why don't you come into the kitchen for a snack?"

Soon they were all sitting happily at the kitchen table, drinking juice and eating the cookies they had helped bake. Everything tasted delicious.

The four friends agreed that this had been the best rainy day ever!